My Father's House

CAL KINNEAR

Taurolog Books
2014

ISBN 10: 0-923980-71-7
ISBN 13: 978-0-923980-71-9

Taurolog Books
Vashon Island, WA
calkinnear@gmail.com

Cover Illustration: The house on the cover was built by my great-grandfather in the 1880s, after he had sold his farm to move to Seattle from Illinois. My great-uncle willed it away on his death, and it has since been razed. The vintage photograph is undated and uncredited.

Foreword:
In a Chair by the Stove

In a chair by the stove

Heraclitus is said to have spoken to visitors who wanted to meet him and who stopped as they were approaching when they saw him warming himself by the stove—he urged them to come in without fear for, he said, there are gods here too.

(εἶναι γάρ καί ἐνταῦθα θεούζ,).

Tonight, winter, it is dark, wind and rain up outside, and I sit by my wood stove reading this sequence of poems I wrote twenty years ago, about my family, about my earliest years, which is to say, my becoming me. Tonight is a Bardo night, near the winter solstice, hours on the border of here-and-there, now-and-then — Bardo meaning "intermission" in Tibetan, a pause, a time out from time. No-time, un-time, between-time. The poems are a sequence of moments brought back not from time but from a mingling of memory and imagination. From Bardo.

Modern scientific thought has demanded we be so certain about time, that it is a line, like a railroad track, on which we find ourselves in a passage we can never reverse. As I reread, as I give way to silence and the rise and fall of the wind outside, I know time, memory itself, is something different. Ghosts, visitations, hallucinations, the reshapings of desire and regret, where do these reside? If time is real and linear, how do we track its reality? Its pastness? Are "reality" and "pastness" not themselves fictions?

I may think I leave the past behind, bring it with me only as a study, something apart from me, an historical and archeological knowledge. Time presses inward on me from what has not yet arrived. Now is a wave I live in the surge of, and is as much after as before.

These poems are the gathered, the stored bones of the past. Bones are an enigma. They seem to be the nothing left behind at death. They carry in their marrow, stored and waiting, the life that is approaching. They are seeds. I keep with me the bones of what has meant the most to me, and passed away. These bones may lie for years buried in patience, until some unexpected moment calls them to life, and they rise, and knock, and there they are at the front door, asking to come in out of the dark and the weather.

This father of mine, born thirty years before me, who died twenty-five years ago, in whose hands I grew up, comes to me now as much a ghost from where I have not yet been. I am daily less sure who I am there in my mirror. This mother of mine, who died fifteen years ago, she is here, a half-light, a kind of aura, in the same space with the woman I love, the woman I live with, the woman with whom I make this late plunge into what will come. And this sister of mine, who never was, who was not born, lives with us in our house, with the mice and the raccoons, outside with the blue heron, and the frogs singing in the night.

Who is he, this man, my father? You will meet him soon, this force so early sweeping into my life. A man filled with his own life, himself drawn powerfully forward into his own future, until the stroke that stopped him. The wave of my own life as I set out, a wave still pulling.

It is warm here tonight by the stove. Time is in slumber, in the dark. Past and future move softly out there, taking shape and shedding it again, hard to tell one from the other. Only to sense the murmur, the calls, the energy.

So many ages of my life at once clamoring together, the whole dark room resonant. My oldest memory, an attic room, in some house, midnight, rain outside, waiting for Christmas. But other years, and so many people. Any moment claimed by the oldest to the youngest. Tonight, I am the oldest. I sit quiet here in the near dark, wind high in the trees outside. I wait for them all to arrive again, for the first time, a youth not of the body, but of the bones singing, the chorus of them all.

And Death? The One who stops everything, or so it seems. The bone-man, the enigma. The witch with her leaves and seeds. Women wailing at the wake. The tricky-man, who makes you test your luck. And there you are, you'll never know, till the One arrives, the Time.

Under His Vigilance

All fates began in the palm of his old tortoise's shell of a hand and spread in rings through the books of all laws that crowded the shelves of his room, floor to ceiling, and on into further rooms, with their maroon leather spines and vellum pages, their embossed and gilded titles in persian and greek and hebrew and arabic and latin, and their fantastically illuminated initials, each volume a summary and compendium of a segment of the ultimate and paternal law that disposed the universe, and included the law of the distribution of grass blades in a lawn, the law of the rippling of sand along the Pacific littoral and the law of the gathering of crows in certain trees at dawn, the law of the weather patterns generated by the ocean current known as el niño in its bearing on coffee futures, the law of the rules of games and the difficult masteries of memory and spartan annealings of character that sway contests of chance because luck is for the witless, the law of free markets and the successful propagation of wealth through parsimony and parturition, the laws prescribing the glacial dignity and soporific magnificence of the assemblies of the factors of the law whose authority climbs unbroken by difficult stony trails to the perilously high drips and melt-pools of the first words from the lips of the first men in their inaccessibly ancient and exalted assemblies, the laws dictating the promulgation of the laws in their most solemn and resonant justice and their inscription by the hands of arthritic spiders, the laws governing the intermitting of the laws and by whom and by what license or benign neglect and with what impunity, the laws of heredity and inheritance and why my sons had better look like me, goddam it, and listen, my sons, there can be only one law properly considered, because there is only one father, goddam it, and that law is, it's all mine and don't you ever forget who it is gives you everything.

One day there he was at his desk, the man who was our father, who had been away at the wars, so we had heard, with his glacial eyes of a Galapagos tortoise and the one who never slept hunched on the back of his chair, and we couldn't move our legs. He was staring with ponderous suspicion at the furnishings of his room, aiming his bullet lamp of an interrogator, asking the way he had asked farmers—What do you call this thing? What does it do? What are you hiding from me? He spoke with the prosthetic gait of a book, and when he spoke, we smelled mint and dust.

He had the voice of a public address system that followed us everywhere, even into the bathroom, even into our dreams, and it was for our own good, my son, because how else would we learn? The requirement for permission to sleep was inspection every night. We lined up at attention by our beds in the attitude of prayer, because the greatest man, my son, came from humble beginnings. The articles of the Bill of Rights, the Gettysburg address, an Our Father, hospital corners, and clean finger nails. The one who never slept prowled the halls at night and under our beds. Dawn was an icy slap of light across the face.

Before dawn there was a noise, a motion that had just stopped, and the whole house went on trembling lightly. Not a single pot of flowers had fallen off the mantlepiece, not a single crystal goblet cracked, not a break in the sidewalk pavement. We huddled under our blankets without a thing to remember whispering furiously what it might have been. Something in us knew, but couldn't say, and their door was closed. It was a question, reverberating like a bell struck with the force of anything unimaginable. It was him come home, our question, and we were going to spend our lives trying to say it, to get the hang of letting it explode from our lips the way it had to be said, the way any powerful name becomes a curse. No answer, just something to live with like a swallowed hook, because you're hungry. Just like that, lying in the dark in bed, knowing we missed it, had to miss it, feeling it there with us, fattening itself, the seed of our inheritance.

After a good dinner he always sat in the dead center of his office with its perfectly square corners and its marshalled regiments of uniformed books in the company of the tireless vigilance of the one who never slept, read his newspaper and took a napoleonic nap. The house braced, sir! in the rectitude of its corridors and doorways with no jokes after nineteen hundred hours, sir! Whole rooms we had grown accustomed to were erased overnight while we slept without even a scar in the wallpaper where the door had been. Our great-aunt who had visions, who we used to find whispering along the halls at dawn, disappeared, and we learned we had invented her. And our cousin the painter who made us laugh, our cousin with his blue fingers who could find the queen of spades in any deck of cards and pluck frogs from our ears, was gone on an indefinite errand, and there were empty chairs at the table, but we sat at attention with our eyes straight ahead, no one must notice.

I learned vigilance with my brothers and sisters. We saw everything, even with our eyes closed. We intercepted the traffic of words no one ever spoke. We studied the sonance and dissonance of voices, and the silences through closed doors. We came to know the cut-crystal ring of the smile that was not a smile and the weeping from deep in the house that no one owned and was like a wind full of rain under the door. I learned to read the damp message my aunt's finger had smudged on the wall by the phone. I shivered when the little gouts of smoke burst from my uncle's shoulder. My father's dead brother who never had enough to eat sat mournful at the foot of my bed playing with a handful of coins, and my grandmother rummaged in my closet at midnight after something lost. In the glassy hours of a rainy afternoon, we learned to trade faces among ourselves. And one morning, washing my face, I found my brother had left his in the mirror by the sink. At the dinner table, we learned to be as inconspicuous as the china and silver. We spoke to one another in a creole of absences, silences, shadows. We knew what we kept to ourselves.

When we sat down on the floor on rainy days with the deck of cards to push our luck with one another, we had a hard time keeping count. The cards flew. We knew we had to be quick or lose. Everything hung on getting in at the right moment and running. We'd start with two and pretty soon be ten or a dozen. The little blonde girl played with such fever, who'd wanted so to be born but the cards said no, the way the cards do. The brother who would have had our father's eyes and hands with secret hiding places and who dealt from the bottom whipped the pace but never won. And the brother who would have been a little slow made it, made it all the way, until the black queen fell. But there was no time for tears in the pace of the game, and the play would rise at last to an hysteria of cards, air full of shrieks and whistles. Then one final cry of triumph, high, the youngest voice, as the last card fell, snap. And we looked up to see what it was, and we had all lost, the cards said so, and why was it lucky that we were here, smaller than we had been, and how few were we, at last?

He was always the winner and that was the way it was. Because goddam it, I'm the father here! He knew the arm-wrestler's fraternal grip that folded my hand into arthritic pain and knew how to use his weight, which of course it was cheating, but who would have called him out on it anyway? He knew all the rules of when Jokers and One-eyed Jacks were wild, and it got you nothing but trouble to look them up. Don't flinch when you look a man in the eye, he said, be a man. And then stared me down however long it took. It was always a game, and there had to be a loser. Nothing personal, sorry, but you have to learn that it costs if you lose, and the discipline of defeat is good for you. So in the subtle catechism of submission, I learned I was never quits, the sentences consecutive, no statute of limitations.

The door closed with a sigh, bearing them away, he in his uniform as dazzling as an artillery barrage, she with the diamond stars about her neck, in a silk ball gown that whirled like a carrousel. And he left his voice hanging like cigar smoke by the door, Behave, or you know what'll be coming to you, and we were alone in the terrifying freedom of the house with only the one who never slept to watch as looming as our shadows waiting for us at the end of the hall. And we whispered goodnight and held hands as we grew smaller all the way to our solitary beds, where I sang myself to sleep not daring to make a sound.

We understood, without anyone ever saying, because whose else would it be? that night-time belonged to our mother whose soft pale hands with the enchanting rings of gold and turquoise smoothed us into our pillows, whose luminous body lingered in the room long after the last murmured syllables of her voice had trailed away taking along the lamp, the window and the door, and there everywhere was the night come from under the bed which no longer rested on anything solid and out of the drawers and the closet to whisper its stealthy business, with its fluttering hands of blind moths searching for our faces, with its beggar voices pressing up wanting so little, a penny, a piece of candy, just one strand of hair, only let us in, we are so lonely in our blindness, and she was very near then, a breath of earth and damp from the folds of her cloak, a sigh, the blue seeds of sleep stirring in their little purse, the flicker of needles beginning to waken in their nest, the sussuration of scissors.

What We Knew

Sometimes we heard crying, but never found anyone, though we went searching from room to room. It was an ancient forest sound of water falling from giant sword ferns, from ghost-gold maple leaves larger than hands, from the thick fallen bodies of cedar trees older than Christ, falling drop by drop through a miasmal, opiate air. It was the ancient, maternal grieving of a house for its freight of stunned souls. All night long, rain fell in milennial sighs, eroding memory to an essential, fine-china bone. The old-woman lavender water and lilac perfume of a funeral trailed away down the hall, and the pall of wakes more difficult than childbirth hung like dead chimney smoke in the living room. For days we languished housebound, stricken by a lassitude like the backwash of a scarlet fever. The most ordinary things we could find to say carried unexpected echoes and nuances, amplified by the nearness of the dead. And it was further days before we could with any assurance sort the living from the dead.

There was going to be a dinner party, and the lace and silver and crystal floated on the polished mahogany depths of the dining table. Don't you dare muss anything, she said, and I knew I would eat alone in the pantry. The ham with its spikes of clove reeked in the oven. The potato water boiled forgotten on the stove. And why was there no air in the kitchen so I could hardly breathe? Our mother stood by the sink over the half-chopped onions, looking at the knife as if she'd forgot what a knife is for. I wanted to say something, if I'd known what it was. It's just the onions she said. Don't ever cut onions without a piece of bread in your mouth. And she sent me to my room until I could stop crying and act my age.

When she thought no one was watching, our mother sat at the kitchen table staring into her hands as if they held an enigmatic and prophetic constellation of black tea leaves. That was when the other women came to commiserate. Not the ones in the pastel frocks with the voices of caged birds, who perched on the edge of their seats and sipped milky coffee from bone china cups. The dim colorless ones who thickened the air like a mist and hovered with the stillness of curtains, whose faces were eroded from the endlessness of grief and whose only names were the names of loss. They were her shame, like a childhood lived in poverty. She hid them among the dust rags in the closet and in the cardboard carton by the washtub reserved for worn-out clothes. They were the secret companions of her solitude, her nights.

In the lulls between the vast wallowing anticyclones of weeping, we could hear ourselves giggle in the folds of the curtains, from the closet, from the next room. We worked out our best plans hidden under tables or slipping out of our rooms to meet on the dark stairways. We ran everywhere. We never let the house rest. A nest of mud and straw grew in the china cupboard and violet-green swallows looped for days between the toaster and the sink, elegant and persistent. Small huddles of mice gathered at certain hours by the glass doors that guarded the leather-bound books of the law. A drift of snow collected in the bathtub. Letters in stark crude strokes of orange and rust appeared in the morning on several doors—a "W" and an "O." It was during this time that the refugees in their cotton pyjamas began to show up passing through the basement. Walls shifted again. Doors came back that we had forgotten, women in dark cotton robes that hid all but their eyes, silent men loitering under the shadows of their hats, with their cardboard boxes of treasure tied with faded ribbons—penny-whistles and panpipes, sheath knives, ivory combs, dyed leather purses, bright-colored plastic animals.

She came to visit her daughter once, from all the way across the country, so we heard, bringing two steamer trunks of clothes and bundled letters, and an air of sage and summer roses and bees. And when we were allowed to visit her where she sat propped among blue satin pillows in her delicate bed like a cameo brooch, it seemed she was as delicate as silk thread with the high, trilled accent of a songbird. Her hands opened for us with their spidery net of veins, and lace cuffs at the wrists, and we saw a tiny stoppered bottle of blue glass which she held to the light so it could sing. And on Sunday she dressed in a dress of watered floral silk and a tiny hat of meticulously stitched flowers with a gossamer veil over the soft powder on her face, and came downstairs to receive, this beautiful young grandmother with her hair so white it shone blue as ice and her collection of glass statues, jewelry, fine lace and elegant gentlemen who appeared at the door bearing engraved cardboard invitations from the previous century, this woman with the hands of water that made crystal out of lamplight, and whispered the cards to her from the green baize, so the casual money from an afternoon of bridge came to rest beside her like a plate of tea sandwiches.

He had drawn with the casual flourish of a man signing his name his own portrait in charcoal, and it hung there in the hall shadow. Nobody mentioned him, nobody named him. He might have been a stranger, this father of our mother, who was dead already a quarter of a century. He was gone like a stone in water, taking with him the brothers she never had, gone when she was only a girl with her hair clipped back beside her ears and the loveliest summer frock you can imagine, already listening with her ears of blood roses to the violin whispers from the corner of the room. He'd left himself like quicksilver in a mirror, this man with a way of tilting his head to wonder and the smile of a fugitive man already rarifying on his way to death. There she stood watching by her mother's side, voice of crystal and silver, who trumped the heart ace with her black deuce. This was my grandfather holding in his reed hands a vase like a fish about to glide away into the shadows of a pool, my grandfather with the pallid, wavery heart of the moon, look, who half rises and turns in his morning coat of dappled light from a long window, his walking stick of cascading water, his dancer's shoes of swirled pools of oil. This is my grandfather the portrait in charcoal, the connoisseur of jars, who left as his dower these silk-fingered women.

We could feel it coming on like a fit of tedium on a rainy day. A plate that had been locked in a cupboard suddenly fell to the floor and shattered. And then there wasn't a sound, and we put our hands over our ears and held our breath like divers plummeting into the sea. Only the one sound, mother, of broom straws and glass. Shadows rushed toward her tumbling over one another with the well-bred orderliness of folded linen, dust balls spun out of the corners, cracks advanced along the plaster in the halls, photographs hung crooked on their hooks and a stain blossomed on a lampshade. One word exploded into the trashcan, the last, the lid slammed down, what was left was a wallowing immeasurable wrong, and the door of your room, mother, sobbed shut and that was all. Then our lips were numb, our hands wouldn't rise from our laps, we sat staring at nothing, we could find none of the names for things to comfort them in a stone-deaf house. And the only sound for days was the chalk-on-slate scratch of our father's pen as he sat at his desk signing his orders.

There are only two kinds of women, he said, the ones like your mother, and the others. And we thought of her on Easter in her white-frilled dress with the layers of crinolines and her white net gloves and the little hat all woven with flowers and the nearly imperceptible veil brushing her faintly reddened lips, and we could hardly see the black fall of her hair. And he never said what he meant, the others, but we heard it in his voice, we knew.

He never touched her in anger, our mother. We knew, we watched from behind curtains and just outside the doors. He hardly raised his voice, and why would he need to, who could draw his voice taut as a silk cord to caress like a paper cut. Her face was a mask of obedience, and we never saw a tear, but she was crying, we knew she was crying by the sobbing of her shoulders. Then she hiccupped once and wouldn't come out of her room for dinner. So we sat alone with him at the table, and I couldn't eat because the overpowering reek of old meals kept breathing out of the walls. And he said Eat or go to your room, so I did. And they told me later how he said we didn't love her enough, that we had to love her more to make up for the ones she had lost, the ones under the dusty sheets in the closed-off rooms we were afraid to go into. So I drew her a picture of a house with flowers, and wrote I love you, I really do. And the next evening our father brought a dozen roses in a crystal vase, and she smiled, and we could almost forget.

At the top of the stairs she stood in her dressing gown of luminous chiffon and her mingled light of angel and mother, her feet barely brushing the top step. And there I was, dumb as a hat-rack or anything else just waiting to see. I knew she could fly and she only didn't, to show me, See, you didn't believe. Then, as if it was the most natural thing, she stepped out and fell all knees and elbows and bruises over every stair-step to my feet. And how was it she was crying then, crying the same way I cried, and I wasn't dead?

The silver tea service with its moon-glow surfaces lay suavely bedded in wraps of flannel, the bone china shone in its shut cupboard like the gleam of teeth, and the crystal goblets stood tall and clear on their shelves, barely containing their bell-tones of trembling light. And there she was already at five in the morning at the kitchen table with the cream smelling of ammonia, polishing the knives and spoons, because it had to be perfect, because it had to shine like the gleaming ebon toes of his shoes. The air steamed with effort, and, Listen, she said making her fury shine, meaning me, Do you think I'm your servant? And she set me to polish water spots from the plates, and scour the pans until I could see my face.

It was New Year, a storm of night to end all nights, and he ordered in a twenty-piece band and the neighbors from all over the neighborhood to watch, and he had rows of benches set along the porch by the window, and bleachers in the archway to the living room, and a table with a punch bowl and sugar cookies with red and green sprinkles, and lit every light in the house. The musicians nearly filled the room with the violin and the bass, the horns and saxophones, the flute and wheezy accordion. In the tiny space of floor that remained I danced an awkward two-step in the arms of our mother like a moth desperate to burn himself while my brother laughed in silent agony from the mantlepiece, and my father seized my sister's hand, folded her in his smell of dust and tobacco and mint and waltzed her until she was fall-down dizzy.

He kept her in a sequestered room we could never enter, our oldest sister, to torment us. We blushed when we thought of her, though we never said we knew. At the bottom of the stairway we'd run sudden into a gasp of anticipation and be struck giddy as though we might faint. Smug-faced cunning boys in the ill-fitting livery of expensive stores appeared in the doorway arms full of packages filled with unmentionable splendors and we knew they were hers. We who put out the garbage, climbed trees, wrestled with one another in the dirt, struggled with our tedious lessons, ached to be let see her. Listen, he said, our father, touching my face with his rough hand, Beauty is truth, and we thought we might have glimpsed her imprint in the air, but it was only a memory of rose and musk caught in the drapery of a doorway. Look, he said holding up a porcelain vase, The flawless line, the perfect tone, how it takes light like pearl. And we listened to the way his breath of a man shortened as he imagined the ripple of her gown, and saw the dense basalt pool of him stir like tar. And look, we knew, he opens the door, and in the dim light from the street falling through the curtains when she doesn't know he's watching, look, the curve of her nakedness as she sleeps unguarded among the bottled scents and powders. And we longed to know too, waited in the dark with eyes half-open, hot with shame, not knowing exactly why, wishing, just before sleep, the door would open, she would be standing there haloed in the hall light.

Our mother came to get her in that particular robe that fell open at the throat so you could see how white, and she led my sister, locked the door, drew the curtains, sat her on the bench and stood behind so they looked into the mirror together, into the bottomless vertigo of initiation. And she said, Look, and showed her the powders in the porcelain boxes, the colored cakes and the tiny brushes, the stoppered crystal bottles with the smells so dense they made you sneeze. And her hands moved like tree branches lifting in a wind, moved as if they moved over herself, so cunning, devising face after face, fashioning the woman out of the girl. And she stood plaiting her hair, saying, Listen, this is our art, to weave nets out of brush strokes and shadow. They languored into evening in the rosewater air, never mentioning that hoarse breathing full of mint and dust, nor the ox-weight of him.

Who is the most beautiful of them all? he said looking down the table at our mother from his paternal siege, that frozen stone of a man with his pale jade eye of a connoisseur and his rock crystal eye of judgment. The jade eye rested with the equanimity of a brooch on our mother's breast, and the crystal eye snapped with a spark of ice, but his hands of a chess player sought out our sister, she was the one, his precious and the beauty queen of the universe. He sat her on his lap, kissed the crown of her head, locked a delicate chain of silver around her neck, and whispered warm in her ear, Now you're my little treasure forever.

She was the Intended, the Vessel, the Prize. They seemed to be born knowing of her, these young men who appeared at the front door without advertisement, in their somber-man suits with their measured gifts and smiles, keeping their hole-cards close. He knew how to make a deal, our father with the eye that would not flinch, if it took a year of Sundays. We hid in the curtains and held our breaths. We watched and saw nothing happen. A negotiation wallowing in the turgid smoke of smoldering tobacco leaves. A deal was going down and it looked like the after-dinner hibernation of bears. Of course you understand he said, striking faint sparks from the steel they kept hooded under the surface of their eyes, In these enlightened times she is wholly at her own disposal. Of course. So they passed her among them like a sample of fine sherry, sniffing, tasting, noting the rich gleam of his name in her, and the faint but visible stirring like a Magellanic cloud about her loins of the clamorous souls of unborn children. And when she came back to visit, we no longer knew her, she wore the perfect hair and dress of a matron, with a rope of cultured pearls and children about her neck.

A Sister, A Brother

I think she had come a long way to see me for the first time, standing there in the hot doorway of my fever room. She half-hid, my little sister, in the ample skirts of our grandmother. She was an old sepia photograph and smelled of mud and garlic and roses. I saw already in her thousand-mile eyes of a wolf that she wasn't here to stay, though I wanted her to kiss me on the mouth, wanted her to caress my forehead with a cool cloth. She took a step forward as if to speak and vanished. My grandmother smiled her benediction of regret for lost things as she went into the closet and shut the door. The rain came then, dashing against the windows, and someone was crying in my sleep, where two tall candles guttered in front of an empty mirror. When I woke, there was another woman who called me Dear and wore a surgical mask and white gloves while she clipped the hair short over my skull. For a century of nights I lay tangled in a knot of sheets and wore boots with the laces tied together, and ate boiled spinach and beets.

My sister, my dear heart, found her ways. She took her fox's scent of a young woman out to run under the moon. The windows watched her through their closed lids of righteous sleep. They acknowledged nothing. They kept the perfect blandness of waiters. We watched her with the eyes of our dreaming, watched her run and pause, sniff the air, jump with sharp glee after invisible birds, range wider. Our bones burned all night like beds of charcoal. Just before dawn she came back in through a chink in her restless sleep, and we stumbled through the next day, already falling asleep in our bowls of oatmeal.

My sister, my deepest shame, with her rag dolls, her chapped lips and her flowered cotton panties. She with my own voice who would always say it before I did, and whose laugh I laughed. And the hand that brushed against mine, meaning, You know. And I did. The way led to a room without doors or windows, a room that the house kept hidden from itself, while our father sat in the living room like the tomb of a Norman crusader with a book of stone pages, his eye of a searchlight sweeping the halls and doorways, and our mother in the kitchen filled with steam, with her tempered knife of german steel, worked at our dinner of carrots, potatoes and a slab of tongue. Our way led by closets and drawers smelling of vanilla and eucalyptus, past the brush of the fox stole with all its gleaming eyes that made us shudder, past the silk stockings and the flimsy lace things, past other objects and devices hidden and unmentionable. And each time there we were at last alone together in our interchangeable shame, sleeping the same dream, waking to the same skin, which was mine, which was yours, which was what we had of refuge.

That sister as close to me as the smell of my own sweat, with the hair that gleamed like spider webs, who could run faster than any dog, who knew the songs of jays and crows, who touched my ear with her tongue when she whispered. That sister, the one I was born to lose. She left one night with a strange man who promised her a rose tattoo. She left her girl-necklace with the charms she'd collected. She took a suitcase with her photos, and the memory of her eyes. She took the keys and doorknobs and the doors themselves. And there I stayed, like the bust of an ancestor on a table, half-bronze, half-bone, staring out on a white morning as flat as a window pane.

Sometimes I had a brother. He stayed with me and shared my room and my bed. He shared my radio. He shared my single unchartable loneliness of Sunday afternoons. I said words I would never have said to anybody else. He was dark and slippery like water in a drainspout. Whenever he was around, things got lost. A tin whistle, a ring, a ribbon. He just laughed the peculiar throaty laugh of the mute, and winked with the shadow of his eye. Losers weepers, he said with his swift hands.

My brother, my rib. What would I have been without him? He was the quickest. He got away with the laughter and hid under the table, hid behind the door. When the flash cameras looked to say Who?! I was the one with the smear of jam on my face. I was the one caught in the leg trap. He was the one knew where the change was in the kitchen drawer. I was the one they found with the coins in my pocket. He was the one found the key to the monkey's cage. I was the one sent under the couch to catch him and got bit. He was the one knew where the makeup was and the little jewelry box. He was the one in the mirror with the eyes of liquid turquoise, mouth of sudden flame, rills of gold spilling from his ears. And I was the one with the slash of grime across my cheek, the skinned knees, doing the hours in solitary, forbidden even to whistle.

It was always me caught, accused, shut up in my room to do time. Me with the light hands, the empty hands. We all understood that, I was the one with all the faces, I was the one with the no-face. I was the one knew everything and stood stone dumb, when he said, Don't you ever lie to me, and I didn't, because what was a lie? I was the place in the hollow tree anyone could leave things safe. I wore my hot face of shame over my face of secrets, smooth and close as a river stone. I sat out my solitary. I-know-what-I-know, that was my treasure, better than the radio, my hours of company.

My brother with the secret knife in the sheath up his sleeve. My brother who rippled like shadow, who went anywhere water went. My brother who made his living as a parodist at stag parties, who borrowed my face the night he ran away, and I didn't know it till I saw in my mirror he'd left me his. He left the front door wide and we found raccoons in the pantry. In the morning, our father woke from a nightmare with a hand-scrawled note clutched in his hand, which he tore in little bits without reading. Next day, men came to put in a new alarm system. But no one could stop the omens—a cat fight at three in the morning, a dead sparrow on the door mat, a spill of salt on the kitchen floor. Forbidden to speak our brother's name, we invented pig-latins and sign-languages based on common gestures of courtesy, and wrote notes in lemon juice.

Every story came with a lesson. It was Christmas. It was time we learned the lesson of giving, my children. If you're going to piss, piss like a horse. The tree in the living room had more lights than anyone's in town. More presents wrapped in colored foils with satin and brocade ribbons. It's all yours, our father said, standing in front of the tree with his arms spread wide, meaning him, like he was running for governor, his body, his house, everything, our inheritance, take. And he took us in his arms, in his wide embrace, his creatures, flesh of his flesh. You give, somebody owes you. You can take that to the bank. That night my brother packed in haste and left, through the basement, through the coal chute, through the dank sewers. Nobody, nobody was going to wrap him up like a lollipop and set him out to sweeten a deal.

So I knew for all of us the story that wasn't even a story because it couldn't find the words among the stolid furniture. And there were no songs, because what could you sing with a single note accompanied by the single string of a ukelele? It was a story that never happened, under the baleful eye of the one who prowled the house in felt shufflers and never slept. It was a story made of things that didn't move. The stolid furniture. The dark drapes. The brussels sprouts and the squash and the asparagus my brother wouldn't eat, night after night, which was the No he was forbidden to say. And all the other words that weren't in any of the books that he hid under his tongue, quick slippery words we weren't sure we had heard right when he spit them out or growled them or sucked them, and we only guessed what they meant or where he'd got them. But we knew the one thing—he was digging with them, mining, sluicing, paring, etching. Infesting the lumbering pile of the house finally like a plague of termites. And still finally no story, only that he went on digging deeper and deeper into himself until finally he was gone, not a syllable, not a faint grimace left to scar the air where our father sat at the head of the table saying, Good riddance to the spoiler! He brought it on himself!

So he was gone, leaving our ears ringing and the heat-shimmer of mirage in the hallway. And when we heard from him next, the scraps of paper were nailed to the door, his ten demands, his eleven theses, his critique of the decadence of privilege, Down with the tyrants and exploiters! He kept on the move trusting no one, a fatigue cap for a roof, and the coarse wool blanket of wool smelling of goats that he slept in. He was a monk in the service of nothing and no man, a warrior armed with the lightning bolt of the void. God was dead, goddam him, and he was what was left, the purity of wind never to rest, never to take shape. He was the quick fire of an indiscriminate acid that ate at himself like starvation. His messages grew shorter, a handful of letters nailed to a board. Then the silence of an empty page, a few wisps of smoke and a curl of flame remembering the intransigent ferocity of his eyes of a condemned man. He had nothing more to say, he would live out his perpetual exile of a recusant. Our father drank nightly vinegar to his oblivion and shattered his name against the fireplace hearth. We kept each a syllable under our tongues like the blood taste of steel, and woke from nightmares of shattering windows and the sudden slash of razor blades.

Forget him, forget his name, he said only once in the same voice that set the implacable clock on the stairway to the atomic number of the sun's core and calibrated the ambient heat to the ponderous tides of his blood, saying, Why is it always cold in here? Then suddenly there was an eraser smudge where even his memory had been. However we went around the house looking, we couldn't find him, there was nothing left. We kept a few things in a shoe box saying they might have been his—a few coins, a penny whistle and a jackknife, a Dodger's hat, the blackened tongue of a shoe. But they didn't make up anyone. We hid in a closet to cry our dumb tears and wore black crape armbands against our skin. And then we understood he'd had the last word after all, the unspoken, the stubborn watchword we couldn't stop hearing after the hammer blow, Forget. He was our martyr who had lost even his name, our knight of no countenance.

The Untouchables

On Sundays we dressed up in our very best clothes, and our father wore his uniform of general of the army, arrayed with decorations and medals going back through five wars of national glory to the grand army of the republic. He was as resplendent as a heaven of fireworks on the Day of Our Independence, my children, when brave men gave their lives for our freedom. And after breakfast he led us through the storerooms where he kept a few things he had brought back from the wars. Cases full of jade bottles, look, the color of algae on a pond. And this gold communion cup Cellini himself must have made. And the reconstructed altar from the ruins of a Tuscan chapel. And here. This helmet with a hole in it and the bayonet of a Japanese soldier. There were more rooms than we had imagined, and we followed, silent as coattails, in the retinue of the bicentennial victor as he smiled, nodded his head, waved his wave of a man of humble beginnings acknowledging his birthright, and, goddam, it took them long enough to give in, my children.

When we went walking in the city, we looked straight ahead. The Toledo steel eyes of our father swept the way with their peremptory command. The ones from whom everything had been taken had earned the gift of invisibility, with their eyes of rainwater misting the air. Asking for nothing, only asking why. With their patience of bakers listening for the leaven to swell. With their swiftness of knives to slice carrots and peppers. With their stink of hot oil and garlic, cumin and ginger and cinnamon. Never eat from the street stalls, he said, as they watched us from their hovels of steam and smoke. It's unclean. It'll make you sick. And we slipped away later to hold it in our mouths, to melt, to find what he meant, unclean.

At first he hardly seemed to notice. This was the great experiment, after all, of assimilation, to see if everyone could become like us. So we went into houses very like ours, for a glass of water and a cookie, Thank you very much! because we knew our manners. But I understood what they weren't telling, and was afraid he would learn. Then we began to notice the others, how many they were, trudging out of newspaper accounts from the other side of the world, wearing cracked shoes or none, carrying babies as shrunken as potatoes. They came washed up on shore, shipwrecked in frail boats, arriving however they could, without permission. Gray people with the language of birds, with the language of cats, who slept under their hats. Stay away from them, he said, they're no good, they're commies, they don't want to work. They had defective lines of fate in the palms of their hands. When we met them in the streets they showed us, See, what can we do? They were born to be losers. Because destiny is ours, my son, showing his left hand of cured whole leather with the maps of our victories tooled across it, It's our fate to win, and, look, somebody has to lose.

Saturdays, we were up before everyone, even before first light, slipping into the attic along the rows of old steamer trunks with their rotting leather hinges, sifting with our hands of thieves through the dark suit jacket shiny as coal at the elbows with the hole in the money pocket, sniffing the flowered frock with the daub of lipstick on the sleeve and the scent of old tears, shuffling into the cracked patent leather shoes with the soles of car tires, scratching a finger on the broken-off point of the clasp knife. And the smell was up there of old cooking—and how did it get there?—mothballs, talcum powder and the pomade men slick their hair with. And, outside the little den of our whispers, the thin high voice of lamentation from the spaces between the walls, whose memory held in a mother's arms all the generations of loss like a sheaf of brown and gold chrysanthemums. Here was the market of abandoned things and no one was buying. Whoever they had been, this was what they left as they went away. Used up, broken. This was ours and forever, the little bit we had to work with. This was our true inheritance.

He indicated them to us with a wave of his foreman's hand. They like gardening and housecleaning, he said, it's what they were born for. With their merciful eyes of stray dogs. They do what they're told. With their patient clay palms, with their fingers of woven grass. Simple people, he said, you have to let them know who's boss. With their hands that whispered when he turned his back, just listen, young master, just leave the basement door ajar. We're stiller than the china lying in its dreamless rectitude, we're less than the shadows of shadows. And of course trying to fall asleep I understood what they meant and lay rigidly still in my sweat-stained bed as they picked over me like delirious ants, carrying off and bringing back through my turbulent nights, teaching the conjugations and moods of twenty verbs for submission, the five genders of the shoal of nouns distinguishing ecstasy from hysteria, the habituative aspect of amatory verbs, the use of the fourth person plural to those beings, secret and removed, who could not be spoken of directly, and the calligraphy of the glyphs they brought me, looming and revolving in the current of dreams.

It is still hard to think of the basement beyond the first step of the stairs. It was the way out, but not like a door. It was where things were delivered and taken away, through a maze of scuttles and traps—milk, coal, garbage and the shiny garments of the dead smelling of moth balls. We found soft dirt in the corner by the wall and, my god! a buried enamel bedpan filled with dolls and jade earrings and sharks teeth and porcupine quills. On certain days women in heavy dresses that swallowed light came to the pool of water in the laundry room to do their wash, and we played hide-and-seek among the dripping sheets. Coal gleamed in a heap by the glowing stoke-hole of the furnace, and we found a narrow tunnel that ended at a pit of bottomless water where pale fish swam without eyes. And when we crouched down very still we could hear breathing somewhere like the breathing of a sleeper very patient and slow, not at all interested in us, smelling of cabbage and apples and mold.

It's just grandma, everybody always said when we heard the rustling in the night. Don't mind her. She was poking in closets and under beds, talking to herself in a soft singsong as she went, looking for something she had put away, oh, months ago, or years, it was so hard to keep track of time, a packet of dried leaves, a brass button, a flicker's wing. All she needed, she had in her apron pocket—a bit of ribbon, needle and thread, some wax. And we turned over and shut our eyes tight, there was nothing to be wakeful about, she had come as far as she had because things were always getting lost, and that was her business, and a good thing too, so many things lost, grandmother, in this bottomless night, if you would only come to us, slip under the covers to lie warm beside us, in our bed of mortal fear.

For years we could still find him in the chancy half-blindness of certain twilights, our grandfather who lived in the highest attic and could call the air-sprites from the winter lightning to dance under the rafters, our grandfather with his startled white hair of a dandelion and his giggle of a boy. He showed us, look, the sawdust heaps at the entrances to the mines of the ants that descended all the way to the basement and beyond to the roots of centuries-old forests. And look, the enormous streaky globe of a gray moon lifting into the very peak of the roof, lit from within by the furious hum of hornets, and the spent clothes collapsed in their narrow cases, salted with little fogs of camphor, it didn't matter, they had found their way anyway, all done with their drowsy voracious midnight hungers now, tucked away in their silky sleep of princesses, the moth pupae dreaming on the faint streams of their transmigration. And once he showed us the shaman-head of an owl and said like this, dance with me, so we danced, and he showed us the small clean bones of voles and wrens and said come with me, and we wouldn't, and he went out the window so quiet we missed it, and that was the last.

When my father took me out, I wore a starched white shirt, gray wool slacks and a bow tie, and the one who never sleeps accompanied us, a platoon of guards in frogged-coats and shakos bearing rifles at port arms. But when I went out on my own, I went through the coal scuttle, I had holes in the knees of my jeans and charcoal smeared over my face, and I was looking for the tattoo-man who lived in a tent of sage and tobacco smoke, thick in billowy clouds. He was a sweet man, a jokes man, a conjure man. He was a market man with baskets of cinnamon and clove and basil leaf, with bolts of silk and satin to touch, with candies and things to drink from colored bottles. He was a laughing man, with his needles—all that little hopping of bird's feet—with all the star-sparks of heaven running over my belly. And he did it a certain way so they could never see, so the little bites sank through and didn't leave a trace, so only I could feel him coiled there just under the skin, that snake of lights, that smallest dragon, with his long cool flank like a caress, that celestial one.

We snuck them in out of the darkness of closets, from behind curtains, through the mail slots and the coal scuttle, because there was something about them, we could feel that and knew the risk. We said Shh, don't wake him, he's napping, knowing that the one who never slept was as vigilant as an inquisitor. So we sat huddled under the blankets in bed with a giddy and conspiratorial air, like soldiers on the eve of battle sharing a cigarette. We listened to the stories of fabulous oases and temples and market towns he had kept hidden from us in the cabinet of proscribed books. With a flashlight, we studied the maps with their impenetrable jungles and waterless deserts, and on the margins the difficult cairns and glyphs of fierce hermetic spirits with densely aglutinated names we struggled to pronounce. And we studied with avid eyes the dim photographs taken with hidden cameras in harims bagnios and boudoirs almost revealing the secret form and musky flesh of courtesans and houris. And we swore them to secrecy, come in, this is our side of the house, the night, you won't need a face here.

Show me your hand, he said, which I was holding clenched behind my back, and he gripped it in his hands of a vice-grip and prised open my shame with its frail scribe's fingers and its palm blank as a sheet of parchment, and he laughed because what kind of a life was that, with no impassioned love, no fatal doorways or cross-roads. And he stopped laughing and gripped me with the interrogation of his eyes, but no, it was not possible, he saw nothing. And I ran away and hid, and yes, I could feel them, they were still there, the tiny star-pricks just beneath the surface, the tattoo-images mounting up from the heart of humiliation, the silent animals, the birds, the first people with their pot of fire, the secret life getting ready to slip into the world.

Death The Itinerant

The halls of the house went round and round like a nurse in muffled shoes whispering over last things. One day, in a room at the top of the stairs, I found an ancient man and woman wrapped in layers of rugs, deafened by the roar of gale force winds and surf. An autumn light of a half-century ago drowsed amid the furniture. In the high chant of wrens and sparrows, they picked over what was left of an old story in a tongue only they understood, more silence then than sound, eroded, elliptical. I recognized the song. It was the song I hear the sea singing under the house, the song of what is left out, water rising in the capillaries of the walls, leaves and buds sprouting from under the shingles.

In the hour of light folding its wings, we sat out with our mother on her patio of ferns and rhododendrons, with the great fallen sails of maple leaves lying about and all around us the bell tones of water falling on water at the beginning of rivers deep in the mountains and the soft mist of a rain coming on bringing the first taste of the salt forgetfulness of the ocean. We wanted to ask what was this that wore away through all the winters still leaving this lace of being. We wanted to ask how everything could come to be so weightless. But there we were in that hour, afflicted with our original forgetfulness of being born, and the taste of the air itself was grief. And we knew one another by the parting touch, the echoes within echoes of the silence of goodbye, a kiss here on the cheek, yes, there on the forehead, yes, passing slowly but finally among us, You were wonderful, darling, such elegance, such delicacy, such grace. It still lingered everywhere and belonged to no one, this grief. We sat further into its evening in the peace of her laughter of a young girl. The flowers came to her gathering around her chair on their bare feet of old friends, the impatiens and begonias, the roses and orchids and gardenias, the hibiscus poised on its long leg of an egret, the final and unending so-be-it of the lilies. Our mother who bore us all, as if we understood what that meant. So small here, like a last gold leaf twirling down the air. Mother of our consolation and peace among flowers. And inconsolable mother of our greed and fury and the relentless sieges of our loves. Mother sitting restless at our feet, eager to be getting on, the last, the youngest of us all.

There were years of extravagant celebration—that is how we remember it—weekly parades in the streets, bugles, drums, bagpipes, and the ponderous, muffled shadows of victorious armies. The furniture was pushed back in the parlor. Our father wore his uniform of uniforms crusted with honors, *primum inter pares* of the officers of the army of the final victory. And the women, ah! We watched crystal and diamond and calm pools of silk with the mute admiration of mirrors. It seemed it was possible to be nothing but transfigurations of light. And then, without a tremor, without a dancer missing a step in the whirl of a waltz, without the flicker of a single candle flame, it all moved off like the grandest ocean liner slipping down the river at dawn in a light rain. We watched, it took years, our faces pressed against glass. Not a sound escaped, not the lament of a violin, no cries of alarm, not a telegram to say wish you were here, all gone away with him. He had floated out beyond reach, merely growing smaller and fainter, no longer remembering securely the names he had given us to call us to him, nor the routes through the maze of that house that had vanished from around him, nor the names of the small wrens who sang outside his window whose songs he could no longer hear, sitting with the gaped-mouth of an old salmon in a pool of wavery light with nothing left but the silent and tedious tours of the bankers, their tires hissing through the rain-sodden streets of gray Mondays, and the waiting.

He kept on, he didn't give up, he knew he couldn't give up. He had grown older than our grandfather, had years ago gone upstairs into the highest rafters of the house where on Sundays we could hear his tuneless voice of an old crow rolling through one hymn after another as if surely holiness was the accretion of endurance, like a crust of barnacles. We never saw him anymore, but the one who never slept dozed on the back of his chair in his study, the doors locked punctually at 9 and the lights went out a half-hour later, leaving us to grope about with candles and flashlights. And when we went out, nothing had changed, not his palm-print in the pavement in the center of town, not the bench he always sat on, not his name still on the street signs, though no one remembered why, or who he had been, and the mountain we could see sometimes on clear days was still named after him, and his name had even slipped into the biggest holiday of them all, the one with the biggest parades and the fireworks that tore open the night sky so that no one slept or dreamed for a week, and the only voice of every leader booming from every loudspeaker with their promises of order and peace and wealth was his.

One day death showed up, who is always just passing through for a few nights, a distant cousin, a little sinister, who helps himself to the last of the roast and tells interminable stories only he laughs at, then is up most of the night with a touchy stomach or an earache walking the halls talking to himself so no one can sleep. When he left we counted the silver and the candlesticks. Our mother took to her bed in her wool shawl of grief, very small and silent against her white pillow. Grandmother who had been dead twenty years turned up with her glasses on the tip of her nose rummaging in the closet for her lost gift. And my god it was a cousin of mine he had touched, my father's sister's son, blond and robust, scarcely grown beyond a boy, with his wife and five children. And almost as an afterthought, as if he had only needed the diversion, our father who had not spoken in ten years, who governed from memory in those days with their light of watery gruel, our father slipped away in the middle of the night, leaving only the faintest impression in the bedclothes. And as it was winter and nothing would hold light, we burned all the candles we had in the living room, and sat in a circle holding hands until the first sunrise of spring.

He was gone, he was gone out of the house taking the house with him, proving that you can take it with you, goddam it, leaving his eye of a tortoise behind like a scar in the air. So I set a great stone, a marker, Here he lies, this is the place where it had stood so long, that house that was his house, and took the words of his name from my mouth and watched in silence as they sank into the raw stone and lay at last motionless. It didn't make any difference. The names of the principal years and the holidays still all included his name. And we hunkered down there together and didn't say anything for a long time, because what is there but memory? And we would have given anything for the simple comfort of a fire.

Reunion

In the space of a heartbeat I have fallen awake into the boundless loneliness of two in the morning. Someone has just stopped crying. The walls hang hushed with the faint trembling of water. Rockabye, my narrow cot sways in its attic loft. Wherever I am, I am here. A whiff of voices drifts up from below. The stairway drops its dizzying way in the great arboreal twist of its banister, all the silent rooms arrayed like coffins in a mausoleum with their polished doorknobs. I'm listening to the song my blood makes, coursing in my ears. The great snaking dragon of lights goes coiling under my skin with the cool caress of death. They are all here, in the transmogrification of dream: family, friends, strangers. They are utterly faithful to themselves, burning from their secret solitary hearts. That is the one law, the great gaiety, the great grief. In this night at the bottom of winter when the sun dies forever, my brother points at me with his finger of accusation, his finger of summary judgment. Everything is as it should be in this night of reunion. All the lights make a single woven fire. This is my inheritance.

Afterword:
The Clock Has Stopped

The clock has stopped

I'm done reading now for the night. Memories come and go, the faces, the moments, fire flaring and settling back. The constancy of a life is an illusion of the habits we build to protect from our inner weather. Is it any less powerful than the weather out there? Gale force winds tonight. The brief hours of sunlight long gone now. Shadows wavering in against the flames flickering in the fire box. Flaring and banking. The power went out an hour ago, fire and candle-light now. The clock has stopped, inter-mission. Father to son to son, like gravity. Only the energy isn't channeled like that. It's wild as this night, turbulent as the ocean. Given, a gift too vast to manage, and still a gift. To make of what I can. Navigation.

You still come to me, from wherever, in great gusts.

This is my inheritance.

Colophon

This book is set in Caflisch Script, and in Bruce Rogers' Centaur,
a typeface originally designed for the Metropolitan Museum of Art.
The titling is Papyrus.

About the Author

Cal Kinnear lives and writes on Vashon Island, in Puget Sound, on
the western edge of North America. Here are ravens and loons.

Memorials

I dedicate this book to my father and mother, George and Caroline
Kinnear, remembering them with deep love. Memory is a strange
power in us, overwhelming, compelling. I had no sister, not even girl
cousins, though I often wish I had. I dedicate this to her and my
one brother, Grant, as well. But the brother these poems remember
is another, imaginary. I dedicate these poems to the magical border
between memory and imagination.

CPSIA information can be obtained
at www.ICGtesting.com
Printed in the USA
BVHW010446150319
542664BV00001B/8/P